PERFECT FORM

Perfect Form

Written by Nicolaas A Gad

Self-published by

Nicolaas A Gad

albertgad67@gmail.com

ISBN: 978-1-7637114-5-7

First Edition: 2026

Cover design by Nicolaas A Gad

Printed in Australia

TABLE OF CONTENTS

ONE

We always wonder what we're supposed to be doing, instead of just being.

"What's next?" Cheryl asked, as she moved the freshly done painting from the desk to the drying rack.

It was good work, but not great. Cheryl only ever painted as a hobby artist, but in her mind, she strived for greatness. This kept her obsessed, glued to pursuing the next task, like a gambler spinning once more in hope that the next one will win.

"Cheryl… dinner's ready," Cheryl's dad called out from downstairs, so she placed her paintbrush into the cup of water on the desk and left to go see him.

"Thanks dad," she said.

"Of course. Serve up," he replied as he gestured for her to get started.

Her father would ask her questions about her day, her art, her life, but she sat there giving minimal answers, as her mind was occupied by what she would do next.

She ate quickly, faster than her dad, and always left the table early after minimal conversation. She felt that eating was something to finish, not enjoy, and that talking about anything other than her focus would waste her mental capacity, which should be saved for more important things.

Her dad watched her walk up the stairs and back to her room, and in his mind he appreciated all she was. He was proud of her art and her drive, and really believed she was destined for greatness. And it was because of these things, he never mentioned his longing for more time with her, and his desire to get to know who she really is.

He cleaned the table for the both of them in silence, every day out of love. And after, he made his way to his bedroom to wind down for the night.

Cheryl continued with her artwork late into the evening, playing with new iterations, and practicing new ways to achieve different results. She thought if she could change something enough times, eventually it would find its perfect form.

Although almost every time, it fell short somewhere. One line was too thick, one angle too sharp, one shape not positioned properly.

This continued until she grew tired, ready to sleep deeply and rest her mind of shapes and angles. And just as she fell from awake to asleep, on the border between the conscious and subconscious, she could see the perfect combination of lines.

Nothing was out of place. No line too long, no stroke too close to the next. In her tired mind she told herself she would remember it as soon as she woke up, and put it onto canvas. Then she fell asleep.

And when she awoke, she did remember she had something important to note down - something that would resolve her endless quest and close an endless search.

She knew it was some combination of shapes, and she could almost remember which shapes they were and in what order they should be, but she couldn't quite remember exactly how it was.

She went to draw on the canvas as much as she could still see in her mind, but what came out was incomplete and unconfident.

How frustrating it was to have been given the answer to her search, but opting for the comfort of sleep resulted in the loss of her dream.

In her frustration, she took a new blank sheet of paper, and drew what she could. She drew as close to her memory as possible, and when that wasn't quite right, she iterated.

She copied the first drawing exactly and altered one line in the way that felt most toward what she remembered.

Her approach was brute force, rather than intuitive creativity. And what resulted was beautiful but sterile. It contained sophistication, yet lacked depth.

At about lunchtime, after spending hours of the morning trying to find the elusive image on the page with her pen, Cheryl left her room to go downstairs.

Her father was in the kitchen, already preparing a slow cooked meal for dinner.

“Day off?”

He chuckled.

“What have you been doing all morning? Hiding away in your room?”

“I’m trying to finish something…”

Her dad waited for more.

“I’ve been trying to find the perfect artwork. And last night, just before I fell to sleep, I saw it. The combination of shapes on the page was nothing but perfect. No line too long or thick. No shape too close or far from the next. Nothing out of place. But as I slept and then awoke, I have forgotten how it was.”

“So all morning you’ve been trying to find it again?”

“That’s right. I sort of remember how it is, but not quite. If I can just adjust and iterate enough times I’m sure I’ll find it.”

Her father waited for a moment.

“When you draw, do you *feel* the artwork when you do it, or is it more like a problem that you feel you can solve with enough attempts?”

Cheryl had a puzzled look.

“What do you mean *feel* the artwork?”

“Like you can feel where the line wants to go, how thick it wants to be. There’s a space for it naturally to fit into. It’s not something to think about, but something to feel into.”

Cheryl had never thought about this before. She tried to understand, and pursed her lips, squinted her eyebrows and nodded.

“I’ll try.”

She always found such direct guidance from her father, and so trusted his word with all of her heart.

She left to her room upstairs once again, and when she arrived she wanted to feel.

How could she feel though? And why had she not felt before?

She sat at her desk; pen in hand, looking at the page.

“Where does the first line want to be?” she asked out loud.

And as she moved her pen close to the page, she could sense: “not there…” and so she moved her pen around over the page. “Not here either… hmmm… ahh here.”

The pen dropped to the page and began making the first line.

It wanted to go in a certain direction, as there was no resistance that way. The force she used on the pen determined the thickness, and she pressed until she felt it didn’t want to be pressed anymore.

There was a sense she hadn’t noticed before. Some inner guidance that spoke silently through the senses.

As she followed this guidance, line after line, shapes began to emerge, in places she saw fit with no fault. And when the artwork was done, it didn’t resemble anything like what she had seen the night before, except it seemed just as perfect, in its own way.

“Perhaps there is no one perfect combination.”

TWO

That next morning, she awoke from a dream of more perfect shapes, emerging from an invisible guidance that led her toward where she didn't know she wanted to go.

She sat up in her bed, placed her feet on the floor where they found their way into a set of slippers, then she made her way downstairs.

"How did you go?"

"I found it… a perfect combination."

"What do you mean 'a'?"

"I felt, like you said. And what came out was perfect. But it wasn't what I remembered."

Her dad smiled slightly.

"Perfection isn't just one thing."

Her eyes changed in a way that signalled she didn't quite understand, but was making space to be able to.

"I don't quite get it."

"A square is perfectly a square, and a circle is perfectly a circle. Both perfect, yet different."

But this didn’t quite satisfy Cheryl’s search. In her mind, a circle seemed a more perfect shape. No corners, no seams, no joins, a singular line. Much more perfect than corners and multiple lines.

Cheryl thanked her dad for his insights, which were always profound yet left room for her to build on.

Cheryl wondered if perhaps the perfect combination she had found wasn't perfect after all. She still believed there was the perfect form to be found, which was singular and alone in its perfection. She wondered if she had found a square, perfectly itself, and even to look at, but not the distilled perfection she was after.

The morning had come again, at the start of a new week. Her father had enrolled her in an art school, advanced for her age, that was far from where she lived. She would spend some weeks there, boarding in its buildings, and study forms and techniques unique to what she wanted to develop.

She pushed her sheets aside and slid from her bed, touching the cold ground with her bare feet. She had already packed the night before, and so met her father downstairs for breakfast.

They ate her favourite foods, bacon and eggs with pancakes, the salty flavours complementing so well with the maple syrup, and when they finished they stopped their chatting for a moment in acknowledgement.

“I won’t see you for some weeks,” her father said, “you know it’s the longest we'll have ever been apart.”

“I know. I’m excited, but I’ll miss being here with you.”

Her father looked at her with love and pride. And with that, they collected her belongings, a suitcase and a backpack, and moved everything to the car.

The trip took all day. Cheryl looked out the window at passing towns and changing fields, and imagined all the people that were living different lives in different places. An ongoing of happenings was everywhere in places she had no awareness of. She wondered how extraordinary some lives must be, and how unfortunate others would be also.

After some time of wondering and day dreaming while watching the outside world pass by, she fell asleep, and before she knew it, she awoke to the stopping of the car.

Cheryl looked ahead out the front window and could see a large and beautiful college style building, constructed of large stone bricks and surrounded by perfectly trimmed hedges and gardens of coloured flowers.

Her dad came with her up a flight of stairs at the front and into the building.

“You must be Cheryl.”

A tall, thin and fair lady with short permed hair and a sharp outfit greeted them with a smile.

“I am,” Cheryl said, agreeing about who she was.

“Perfect, come this way,” the lady said without introducing herself, as she closed her hands firmly and turned for them to follow.

They walked through the building, the inside exquisite and with artwork that neatly hung from the walls. Each room they passed was themed differently, from detailed realism to abstract shapes open to interpretation.

After several long corridors and past rooms of differing natures they came to a door that seemed more plain than the rest.

“As I understand it, you are seeking something most other artists fail to believe exists,” the lady said.

“How do you know that?”

“Your father told me. You are looking for perfection, not in any form, but in the single and only most perfect form.”

“I’ve seen it, so I know it exists.”

“How did you see it?”

"In a dream. It was right there, and nothing could compare to it."

"Inside this room, we hope you will find it again."

She opened the door that was in front of them, and inside was a large space. It was big enough for a hall of people to fit inside, with high ceilings, and wider and deeper than a single person could ever need. And at the back of the room, the entire wall was glass, behind which was a view overlooking all of the gardens, the forest beyond, and a lake in the distance that sat in front of mountains.

The walls were a perfect white, undetailed in any way, and the floor a black carpet that left no way for distraction. The only thing inside the room was a single white desk at the centre, tiltable to any angle, and a single set of black pens of different thicknesses.

It was hyperminimalism.

"This room leaves no room for influence, no detail for distraction, and only inspiration that nature can provide."

"What about the gardens I can see, with obvious human placement?"

"This is to remind you of the collaboration between humans and nature to create something beautiful."

The lady turned to Cheryl's father.

"I suppose this is it then," Cheryl's father said, "for some time at least," as he understood it was his moment to leave.

"I'll see you soon," Cheryl looked up to him as she spoke.

"You will."

He hugged her tightly, and gave a kiss on her cheek, before turning and walking toward and out the door.

"I'll give you some time to settle in," the lady said, and also soon left.

Cheryl sat at the desk for some time, staring at the page, then out the window, then back at the page.

'How can I find what is perfect?' she thought.

She began by placing a single dot at the centre, and stopped to admire its placement.

"It's not right," she said, as it clearly obstructed the blankness of the visual.

She turned to another blank page, and placed a dot, this time further in the corner so as to not obstruct any of the blankness.

“That’s not right either.” She noticed the weight of the page was now skewed toward the side of the dot.

“Perhaps if I even it with another…” she said as she placed another dot on the opposite side.

“Very plain.”

She tried again to remember what she saw in her dream. Asymmetrical, and detailed, yet it was perfect, she remembered.

And even if she did remember it exactly, she wondered: how could the imprecision of a hand, operating within physical laws, copy down exactly the strokes of that perfect form?

THREE

“It feels as though as soon as a mark is made, imperfection arises,” Cheryl said to the lady as she returned to the room after some hours.

“I have someone I would like you to meet,” the lady said.

In walked a man, probably in his sixties, with an aged yet wise face and long grey moustache.

“This is Phil, he has been working on the same problem for over forty years. When he was young, a bit older than you, he had a similar dream. The perfect form, as he remembered it, appeared before him just as he fell to sleep. And when he awoke the next morning, he tried to remember, but couldn’t quite grasp the full picture.”

“Nice to meet you Phil,” Cheryl politely said, extending her hand out to shake his.

“Pleasure,” he responded, as he reached his hand to meet hers in greeting.

“He will be your mentor,” the lady said, “I’ll let you become acquainted.”

Phil and Cheryl were left in the room to discuss and collaborate on what was in common between them.

“So you came here a long time ago?” Cheryl asked.

“Forty three years, my father dropped me off after a long journey. I’ve been here ever since.”

“You’ve never left?” Cheryl asked with surprise, not knowing how someone could be in that same place for so long.

“My father never returned for me, and so I stayed,” he said, “and continued to work on the problem.”

“Do you remember your dream?” Cheryl asked with high inflection.

“As the years have passed, it’s faded more. Like remembering a memory, it eventually transforms away from what it was originally. I would like to hear about yours.”

“I fell asleep some days ago, and just as I did, I saw a page, and on it were strokes of perfect thickness, balance, curve, that created shapes that fit all so neatly together. There was not one thing out of place.”

“Where did it start?”

“Here,” Cheryl said, as she placed her pen on the page to the left somewhat, with an intensity that created the thickness she remembered.

“And where did that go from there?”

“Up and to the left, I remember,” she said as she recalled the direction in her mind, and moved her pen in that direction.

“And then?”

“And it curved here, and down, and overlapped just once at this point, before making its way to here where that line stopped.”

“Have you come this far before?”

“Yes, I remember another shape began here, and ended here,” she said as she drew the second shape with as much precision as she could.

“And what is stopping you from finishing?”

“I can draw the third shape also, or what I can remember, but there is a depth to it that I cannot quite get right. It is as if no matter how I draw it, with curve to the right or left, or even a straight line, I know it is neither of these, as it is all of them at once.”

“How can it be all at once?”

“It is as if it is a direction other than what the page allows.”

“Behind the page, or in front?”

"Neither of those either."

Phil sat for some time, thinking, as he understood just from this, why he was unable to solve this problem in all his years of working on it.

"As I understand it," Phil began to explain, "the page has two dimensions. Left and right, and up and down. That is what we are bound to with this medium."

"That's right," Cheryl agreed.

"And if we were to somehow draw in the space above and beneath the page as well, that would add a third dimension to work with."

"That's correct."

"But even this doesn't allow for the line we need to complete the artwork."

"I feel that's the case," Cheryl said.

Phil had a difficult time understanding this, however it reminded him of something that he had forgotten, as conceptually it was so foreign to him that it faded because it didn't fit into the world he knew.

"I met another here at this place some years ago. One night we shared a dream, of a colour that doesn't exist. One new, and so different from all the rest, but once I saw it, it seemed so obvious to be something that exists," he explained.

"What was it like?"

"Impossible to explain, or compare to anything. We discussed it for days afterwards, trying to describe its nature, its deepness, vibrancy, shade, hue, but nothing could truly describe the experience of it."

"What happened to the other person? Are they still here?"

"They worked on this problem for years also, while I worked on mine. But I haven't seen them in a long time. Perhaps it was solved. But it wasn't my area, and I put all of my attention into my own field."

"These seem like impossible problems," Cheryl said.

"Impossible in this world maybe, but not impossible in the mind. I'll leave you to think for some time, maybe you will find a new approach."

Phil left Cheryl in the room to ponder alone again. She sat, frustrated at what she now faced. With only a flat piece of paper, how was she supposed to demonstrate something that required more?

FOUR

It was dinner time, when a tray was handed to Cheryl by a man at the door. On it was a selection of meats, fruits, vegetables and cheeses. She brought it over to her desk, where she moved the paper aside and placed the tray on it.

As she ate she watched the sun setting over the horizon out the window, reflecting an orange onto the lake and leaving the trees as silhouettes of the forest. And when it receded behind the earth, stars began to illuminate in the sky above.

"I wonder how I would describe this to someone who had never seen the colour orange, or never understood what distance means," she said to herself.

Soon she was full, and found her way over to a door next to the entrance, where inside she could shower, brush her teeth, and sleep in a bed that had been made for her.

So much was on her mind from the day, all from breakfast with her dad, to new ideas of concepts she couldn't quite understand. She drifted from a waking state to sleep, where she dreamed of characters in a place that felt like home.

They asked her questions she did not know the answers to.

“If negative one is left of zero, and positive one is right of zero, what one is above zero?”

“What is it?” she asked the character.

“It’s obviously psegative one,” they said, as she awoke on the word ‘one’.

She yawned, and stretched her body to awaken it, before rolling out of bed and looking at herself in the mirror.

“Psegative one?” she asked herself, and shook her head to get it out of her mind.

Cheryl was excited that day to be back working on the problem. How fascinating it was to be on the frontier of something undiscovered. However as she worked from morning to night, and consulted with Phil for more insights as to how to approach the solution, she felt she had made no real progress.

The days passed like this for the first week. Working all day at what seemed impossible, and sleeping at night to strange dreams of foreign questions. That was until the eighth day that Phil mentioned something that sparked a change in her perception of everything.

“When you imagine the perfect artwork in your mind, and you can see it there, where is that?”

"On a page," Cheryl said, "in front of me."

"No but where is that page?" Phil asked.

"It's on a desk, in a room, in my house..."

"That's not what I mean. Let's say you think of a triangle..."

"Mhmm."

"Can you see it there in your mind?"

"I see it," Cheryl responded.

"Where is that?" Phil asked.

"In my mind?"

"But where is that?"

"In the imagination?"

"Where is the imagination?"

"In my brain?"

"So if I cut open your brain, I will find the imagination in there?"

"No... I guess, I mean... I don't know where it is."

"And so that perfect form you saw in your dream, where is that?"

"I'm not sure. Some other place. It's hard to put my finger on it."

"What about a colour that we see? If you look at that pink flower out the window, where is that pink?"

"On the flower."

"If I zoom in on the flower, cut it open, take it apart, where will I find the pinkness?"

"On its cells perhaps?"

"But if I look into the cells, if I look at the atoms, when does it stop becoming pink? What is the substance of the pinkness?"

"Is it just our perception that makes it pink?"

"That's right. We perceive it as pink, but that doesn't mean the pink exists anywhere but inside our minds."

"And so where is the experience of pink?"

"Where is the experience of anything?" Phil posed to Cheryl.

She sat for some time and thought. Is everything inside the mind? But how could it be, if she perceived it as over there? How could what is external be internal at the same time?

Whilst Cheryl was young, she could grasp abstract ideas, and absorbed concepts like these like a sponge. Not only did she understand them as ideas, but she could implement them into her world view, and lived them as a part of her experience.

And so from that day onward, whenever Cheryl looked at a tree, she understood that tree to be a part of her - a construction of her mind. She now lived in a world that had a dream-like quality. It was somehow non-physical, while presenting a physical existence.

And with this new world view, she was able to approach her problem in new ways.

FIVE

“Perhaps the final line is imperfect because we perceive it as so,” she posed to Phil one week later.

“But it is still two dimensional… too few dimensions to achieve what we are after,” Phil replied.

“But perhaps seeing its other dimensions is a matter of our perception, not of the line or paper,” Cheryl said.

“Perhaps that is true, as difficult as it is for me to understand. And how do you suppose we change our perception of it, Cheryl?”

“I’m not sure yet,” she said, only understanding how to get this far.

The problem was once again at a stand still. What seemed like a problem to be solved on the page was now one to be solved in the mind, so she thought. And if that was so, then it would have to be solved in everyone’s minds, not just her own.

How can she first learn to perceive in ways she never had before, and then inspire that ability in others?

She sat at her desk for long days staring out of the window at skies of dawn and sunsets over the lake. She watched the trees gently blow in the forest, flowers grow and clouds come and go. She observed for many days without touching her pen.

And as she stared at the forest one morning, three weeks after she had arrived, she asked a question she had never thought to ask before.

“Why is it so that the trees seem so small from here?” she asked herself.

“Because they are far away,” she answered in another voice, acting as another person.

“But why is it that things seem to get smaller the further away they are?”

She heard the door open, and Phil arrived to her room with tea and biscuits.

“What is the question?” Phil asked, only hearing the last part of what she was saying.

“Why is it that things seem to get smaller the further away they are?”

“That’s an interesting question, Cheryl, and an important one,” Phil said. He paused for one moment, recalling something he had not thought about until now.

He continued, “I once met a man that was blind since birth. He was born that way, without any understanding of vision. He had no concept of colour or shape in the way we do. And as we talked for hours about perception, beauty, the world, we stumbled upon something.

I tried to explain to him that when something is further away, it seems to become smaller, but he couldn't understand it. He could listen, and hear what I explained, but for him with no reference, it was a totally foreign concept.

'How can it become smaller?' He asked me, 'it has a fixed size, it is what it is, it has the mass it has.' I explained it didn't actually become smaller, but that it just appeared to. 'How confusing that must be,' he said, 'how can you know then if something is just small or far away?'

I told him we just can. Our perception of a three dimensional world allows for that."

"How strange," Cheryl said, "something that seems so obvious can be so foreign if you've never experienced it."

"Exactly," Phil replied.

Cheryl again looked out the window at the trees in the distance, so small that they allowed her to perceive depth. If it wasn't this way, she thought, everything would appear flat. It seems the shrinking of something in one dimension allows us to perceive its distance in extra dimensions.

She knew that this insight was somehow important for the final line in her artwork.

Now with some intention as to how to progress, Cheryl took her pen for the first time in days and attempted the line again.

At first she pressed hard to make the start of the line thick, and slowly released the pressure as she drew so the middle of the line was thinner, before pressing harder again so that the other end was also thick.

When she finished that line, she looked at it, and could see that it appeared to, in her perception, recede away from her in a curve. It seemed to become more distant into the page, and then come back again. There was depth.

But it only appeared that way, and it still lacked the dimensions she envisioned. She had managed to add a three dimensional appearance to the artwork, and while it was closer to her dream, it was still not complete or correct.

She wondered, how could she add that other characteristic that was needed to complete the work? How could she step beyond where she now is to create the effect she needed?

She put the pen down, content with this next step as one towards her goal, and stared again out the window as the sun had just receded over the horizon.

No stars came out that night, as clouds blanketed the sky, and soon rain began to fall, leaving long streaks along the windows. She watched as many streaks moved parallel, and some converged and collided, creating larger drops.

And as she watched, she noticed a single streak form as a drop made its way down the window. She identified it appeared to have one dimension from where she was, but when she got closer, she could see it had width, and depth, and volume. It was three dimensional in reality, but only appeared as one dimensional from afar, and when looked at as a line.

And as the streaks continued to fall and her eyes followed them down and out of view, her eyes closed, and she fell into a deep sleep.

SIX

She awoke the next morning, still at her desk, head hazy from rain, and looked out at fresh sky. The land was rich from being nourished the night before.

She got up from her seat, stretched, and made her way over to her room to drink some water, wash, and brush her teeth. And when she finished, she came back into the main room to find Phil and the lady present and talking.

“Your dad is here to get you,” the lady said.

Phil looked disappointed. “You were making such progress, it’s a shame. I hope you will return.”

“I… but I’m not ready, I’m so close,” Cheryl said.

“Your father insists,” the lady said, “I’m sorry, I hope too that you will return.”

And with that, they showed her out of the room, through the hallways and passages that led to the front where she had entered.

Her father stood there, excited to see her with open arms, and she ran to embrace.

They drove home the same way they came, and on the way Cheryl explained of all her insights, of Phil, the story of the blind man, the task ahead, and her progress.

“I’m not finished there yet,” she said.

“Do you want to go back?”

“I do, soon if I can,” she told her father.

“Of course,” her father said, “in time, but soon.”

After little conversation that followed from that, and long hours of watching out the window once more, they made it back home.

The following days Cheryl spent how she did before she left. She stayed in her now seemingly small room at her own desk, uninspired by what surrounded her, and stared at blank pages attempting to draw the impossible.

She understood now that she didn’t need to repeat the drawing each time, only to practice that final line, so when she got it right, she could do the same to complete the picture.

Her pen was basic but usable, her desk imperfect but flat enough, and her room artificially lit but illuminated at least.

With what she had at her disposal, she began drawing line after line. Some with more thickness at the ends than others. Some with the thickness in the middle. Of different lengths. She attempted differing strokes and techniques to see if any would be a direction outside of what she normally could draw.

It was until she drew inward. She started with a dot, and focussed her attention on it to see the inward direction of that dot. It was the place at the centre where the dot got smaller and smaller inside itself - like looking into a tunnel, infinitely approaching a finite and exact point.

She saw that as the direction she needed to go. It was a way that was unlike any of the other ways she had tried. And as she focussed on it, and attempted to move her hand toward her focus, she noticed it receded inward into seemingly nothing.

She watched the pen become smaller in her perception, and then her hand extend in that inward direction also.

She made sure to not break her focus, to not lose this direction. She understood her perception of it needed to remain intact for it to exist.

And when she completed the line, and lifted her hand, it returned back to above the page like it normally would.

She looked down, and saw a line, not up or down, left or right, and not underneath or above the page. It was an inward direction from any three dimensional viewpoint.

It was a new lattice. Something that her brain could hardly understand, but could perceive. It appeared divine in this way, unlike from the existence she knew.

She wondered if others could perceive it as well, or if only she who had stretched her perception so far recently could see such a thing.

She called out to her father, who remained downstairs cooking dinner at this time, and he answered her call.

“Yes?” he said.

“Come here, I want to show you something,” she said.

She heard his footsteps climb the steps and reach her room, where he entered and walked over to her.

She just stared at the line, waiting for him to see, and he followed her gaze and looked down at the page.

There was silence for some time. He was in awe, not quite understanding what he was looking at, with a puzzled look on his face.

“What is that?” he asked her.

“The final line to the artwork,” she replied.

“But how… where is that? How is it possible?”

"It is a new direction, I have discovered," she said.

He stood for a long time, not knowing what words to speak, and after some minutes of admiring this otherworldly depiction, existing in the reality he stood, he put his hand on her shoulder and lightly shook it in pride.

No words needed be said, just that shake and the firmness of his hand told her how he felt. He looked into her eyes with pursed lips.

"We'll get you back there, today," he said.

She packed her things again, all she needed for her stay, and they left at once.

Again she watched the world outside, now familiar with each town and many of the houses she liked the look of along the way.

They approached the front of the establishment, gardens as bright and intense as ever, and bricks looking just as she remembered them days before.

They walked the stairs again, and spoke to the lady at the front, where Cheryl's father stopped for a moment to look Cheryl in the eye.

“Get it done,” he said to her, “and I’ll see you soon.” And with that, he walked out towards the car again, leaving her with a feeling of empowerment and pride.

SEVEN

The lady led Cheryl again back down the passages and hallways toward the plain door of her room. She entered, without the lady, to find her desk exactly as it was, and on it sat a perfectly blank piece of paper, with the pen she would use sat next to it.

She sat, looked out of the window at the lake, forest and gardens, took a deep breath, and then back at the page.

She began to draw the artwork exactly as she remembered. Everything until the problematic line.

Her pen touched the page and moved up and to the left. It curved, and then moved down, and overlapped just once, before making its way to the point where that line stopped.

She drew the second shape as she did before, and found its ending also.

She then pressed her pen onto the page and followed all of the third shape as well, and when she reached the point of the final line, she focussed her perception on it in such a way that allowed her to draw inward. Her hand receded into nothing again, and she moved it until it found its end also, returning back to connect to the very beginning of the artwork.

She lifted her hand, and admired what she had done.

“It is perfect,” she said, as relief washed over her body, and divine beauty unlocked in her mind at the impossible appearance of the shapes.

The sharply dressed lady entered the room some time after, and approached the desk.

Her face turned in confusion as she looked at the page, in a strange admiration, and then awe as she began to realise the impossibility of what she was looking at.

Phil also entered some time after, and saw both the lady and Cheryl staring at the page in trance. He also approached, and as the page came into his view, a sound of quiet astonishment came out of his mouth.

“Oh…” he muttered, unable to find words for what he felt, “just as I remember,” he said, “it’s been so long.”

After some time of staring without speaking, the lady and Phil looked at each other, unsure of the next move.

“We must protect it,” Phil said, “and ensure others get to see.”

The lady left the room briefly and returned with what appeared to be a picture frame, bordered by metal and with thick and tough glass on the front. Inside was padding of a special type that would protect the contents from any trauma.

“This has been unused for far too long in this room,” the lady said.

She pulled from her pockets a set of gloves that she donned, and carefully lifted the artwork from its corner off the desk with calm precision, and delicately placed it into the frame, locking the back.

“This frame was designed decades ago, engineered to protect its contents from almost anything. It is what we use for every special artwork that comes out of this establishment.”

“And what will come of the work?” Cheryl asked, wondering where they will take it.

“It first appears before the director, and is then displayed in the gallery. Works like this are priceless, but for the right number, collectors are then able to purchase artworks from the gallery.”

“How could you put a value on this? How could you let it be hidden away by some private collector? This kind of art changes the world. It changes reality.”

“Reality is not meant to be changed. And it is not up to me,” she replied.

And with that, Phil and Cheryl watched the artwork recede out of view as the lady carried it toward the door, and as the door shut behind her, it was gone.

"The artwork is repeatable, only by me, and at home I have a line of the same nature on a piece of paper in my room. Just because she has taken it, I'm not worried," Cheryl said.

Phil smiled slightly with relief.

"I can't believe you've done it. What I never achieved in forty years you have done in under a month."

"Without your forty years I'm not sure I would have been able to do what I did," Cheryl said, sharing some of the credit.

Some days had passed, and Phil and Cheryl discussed in that time what might happen with the artwork, what price it may be sold for, what kind of person could afford it, and what other mysteries may come from a place like this.

Cheryl's father returned and joined them for some time also. They were well looked after, including dinners of fine food, comfortable quarters for living, and an invitation to the gallery.

EIGHT

A viewing was occurring on the Friday of that week, where prospective buyers could inspect the works. And when they attended on the morning when it opened, they walked inside to view a large room of open space, with only the outside walls hung with the same type of frames that Cheryl's artwork was placed in.

Phil, Cheryl and Cheryl's dad all entered together, now acquainted after the previous week's time together.

"A tea for the viewing?" A waiter asked, and they agreed, taking their cups and walking respectfully to the first artwork.

"The Big Small," it was titled. They gazed through the thick glass at what was on the page.

It was a black circle, totally filled in, appearing as a dot. But they couldn't tell if it was a finite point, a small singular dot, or whether it filled the entire page. It appeared as both big and small at the same time, neither and both at once. It was indescribable in terms of its size.

They sipped their tea and stared for a long time trying to understand it.

"I don't know how to describe it," Phil said.

"Very confusing. Is it big or small?" Cheryl's dad asked.

"Both, and neither. A size that doesn't exist," Cheryl said.

"Hmm," Cheryl's dad said in acknowledgment and slight astonishment.

They moved on to the next piece of art, and again stared for a long time before speaking.

"The infinite straight," it was titled.

It appeared as a perfectly straight line, with no curve, that somehow rejoined itself to have no ends. It created a self contained shape, like a circle, but very much unlike it with no curving line to allow it to exist.

"Now how is that possible?" Cheryl's dad again couldn't help but ask the others.

"It's beyond my field," Phil said.

"Beyond mine also," Cheryl agreed.

They continued along observing and trying to understand many seemingly impossible works, until they reached one that Phil recognised immediately.

"I had a feeling he'd done it," Phil said.

The others admired the work in front of them, that unlocked a whole new area of perception inside their minds.

"I've never seen such a colour before," Cheryl said, "it's so… unlike any other."

"It's sort of… well sort of like nothing else, my mind wants to compare it but it can't," Cheryl's dad said.

Phil just stood with a smirk of pride and remembrance. "This is what I saw in that dream I shared," he said, "it makes me so happy. I wonder where they left to after they accomplished it."

His eyes watered somewhat, feeling a wave of emotions from everything in the room.

And finally, at the end of the walls, in the last frame, was Cheryl's artwork.

Titled "The Perfect Form," it hung with reverence.

And as collectors began to arrive, and made their way from one side of the room around to the ending, they accumulated at Cheryl's work, hanging onto it with their gaze, and drawn to its divinity in a trance.

NINE

Many of the collectors from that day wanted it. It was hard for anyone to put a value on such a piece, and as word spread among those in the know its increasing demand drew the price upward to levels unseen before.

The academy decided on a private auction, and only months after its creation it was sold for an undisclosed amount to one of the wealthiest families in the world residing in the Middle East.

Phil had no intention of staying at the academy as his work there was done, and Cheryl returned home with her father with new knowledge and perspectives, and enough money from her share of the sale to change her and her family's life for generations.

However abundant and rich her life had become though, she never once heard in public discourse anything about her discovery of this new direction. No mention of the artwork she had created, or colours that didn't exist. It seemed these things were well kept secrets among the most elite circles.

She sat in her loungeroom of a new and modern home, with minimalist white interior that left room for thought. On her table she drew on a sheet, inward lines, one after another, producing entire artworks in the dimension no one else could.

And after each artwork was complete, she secured it into a frame and hung it on a wall of her home.

After many months, her home's walls were full of these pieces. And as she ran out of room, she began to place them leaning against the walls underneath those that were already hung. And finally when she believed she had enough, she took the pieces out of her home and into the back of a van out the front.

“You ready to do this?” her dad said from the driver seat.

She nodded with a smile of excitement.

They drove first to nearby landmarks, famous places tourists visited. At the most frequented locations of their country, they hung a piece at each. And when they had exhausted worthwhile locations in their homeland, they crossed borders and continued to hang a piece in each of the world's most popular attractions.

At some, tourists would look in confusion, not quite understanding what they were looking at, and turning their heads to change angles in hope to see more of it. Sometimes individuals would take them down and take them home. Some destroyed them believing it was not meant to exist.

Museums like the Louvre quickly removed the pieces outside their establishments and hung them inside, behind bulletproof glass.

Some at religious locations, as in the Vatican, became places of worship. Candles were lit and lines of people gathered waiting to be in the presence of the works.

Eventually, all of five hundred pieces were scattered throughout the world. Some hidden in people's homes, some still where they were hung, and some taken to locations for public display.

No one knew who hung them, what they truly represented, and how they were made. Scientists studied the pieces, comparing the direction of the lines to that of a black hole - inward in a way that created a new space.

It wasn't until some years had passed and the mystery became something of an enigma that Cheryl decided to become vocal on the matter.

With her resources she organised a conference, inviting the most notable figures in the modern sciences, religion, and media. In her invitation she explicitly stated she would reveal details about the artworks that left the world confounded years earlier.

And on the day of the event, as people of significance from all over the world arrived in a large hall fit for thousands of people, she stood there on stage with a single easel and large piece of paper clipped to it.

When all was settled, she spoke into a microphone clipped to hang in front of her mouth, that broadcast clearly and loudly.

“I understand on this sheet of paper, I can draw a line from here to here,” she said as she drew a line from left to right, “or from here to here,” as she drew a line from up to down. “I also understand if the medium allowed, it would be possible to draw a line from in front of the artwork to behind it, here to here,” she said as she signalled a line going from in front to behind the artwork.

“But what about from here,” she said as she placed her marker on the page, “to here,” she said as she drew a line inward in the direction that was unlike all others.

Gasps filled in the audience, then small chatter and shock filled the room. There was a sense this was a pivotal moment in all of history.

“It was you!” someone screamed from the audience.

“It was me,” she agreed. “Some years ago I had a dream, of an artwork so perfect it couldn’t be described. I worked for one month in the finest establishment to uncover a secret no other had learned before. My goal was to share it with the world, as I believed it to have some significance in understanding our existence, and how we move forward from here.”

“That’s not true,” someone yelled, “you weren’t the first!”

"What do you mean? Come up here," she said to the man, inviting him on stage.

As he made his way up, his body language spoke of nervous confidence.

"I've been an independent journalist for close to thirty years. Close to the beginning of my career, I investigated an artwork that was dated to be at least hundreds of years old. It was unknown about, hidden from the world, a thing of mythology, disregarded by anybody in modern science as fantasy. But I found it, hanging in an elderly woman's attic. It was only a single line, in the same direction you have drawn yours, framed and preserved perfectly. And in the corner, it wrote, 'copied from a deteriorating artefact to preserve its existence.' The lady that owned it said she believed there was one before it, perhaps thousands of years old, that it was copied from, and who knows before that."

"Liar!" someone yelled from the audience.

"Let him speak!" someone else called out.

"I published the finding, but it was categorised as a work of fiction, and never gained the attention it deserved. I'm sure the lady must have passed away by now, and who knows where that artwork has ended up. But what I know from it, is you weren't the first, and for some reason until now, knowledge of this has been kept away from the public for thousands of years."

As the conference came to a close, and reporters and scientists left in astonishment, with work and stories that would make their career, Cheryl noticed something on the piece of paper she had just drawn.

A sphere of a particular size, white in colour and seemingly made of light, made its way from the direction the line drew toward their world, and out of the page.

When it reached the edge of its direction and transversed over into the space in front of the easel, it grew in size, then shrunk, and then grew.

It was undefined in size in this way and floated as if un-influenced by the laws of their reality. And just as it appeared, it receded back into the page, disappearing out of view as it became smaller and smaller in that inward direction.

Cheryl was the only one to see it, as all had left the hall and she remained alone on stage.

“What was that?” Cheryl asked out loud.

She reached her hand into the page to follow where it had gone, and as she did, she noticed it appeared again in the distance of the direction, as a small white sphere.

She waved at it, and it waved back by increasing and decreasing its brightness in flashes.

She signalled for it to come closer to her, and it did. She spoke to it, asking its nature.

"I am from the place above your plane. A place with dimensions extra to your own. I see all of your world at once. I am where you would call everywhere at once. I can do things you would deem impossible. Many of your people have names for me, have worshipped my kind, but I am not your creator. And in that we don't know where we came from, you and I are the same."

Cheryl stared into its centre, listening and feeling the words that it spoke. She understood what it said, and when it signalled for her to follow it, as if it would show her something she needed to see, she reached both of her arms into the page and dove in that inward direction.

She began to fall, becoming smaller and smaller as she made her way down toward a place she didn't know she could go. From the hall, she seemingly disappeared into nothingness, and as Phil returned to check on Cheryl, he noticed an empty room.

"Cheryl? Cheryl," he called out, to no answer.

www.ingramcontent.com/pod-product-compliance
Lightning Source LLC
LaVergne TN
LVHW020657100826
845148LV00012B/2543

* 9 7 8 1 7 6 3 7 1 1 4 5 7 *